DON'T DO THAT!

by Tony Ross

Crown Publishers, Inc. • New York

Published in the United States by Crown Publishers, Inc.,
a Random House company, 225 Park Avenue South, New York,
New York 10003

Published in Great Britain by Andersen Press, Ltd.,
London, in 1991.

Crown is a trademark of Crown Publishers, Inc.

Manufactured in Italy

Ross, Tony.
    Don't do that! / by Tony Ross.
        p. cm.
    Summary: Nellie discovers why people say "Don't do that!" when
her finger gets stuck in her nose and all kinds of people try
to help her get it out.
    [1. Behavior—Fiction. 2. Nose—Fiction.] I. Title.
PZ7.R71992Do 1991
[E]—dc20   91-9347
ISBN 0-517-58575-8   10 9 8 7 6 5 4 3 2 1   First American Edition

Nellie had a pretty nose.

It was so pretty that it won pretty nose competitions.

It was so pretty that Nellie was given a part in the Christmas play, with Donna and Patricia, who had pretty noses too.

"CHILDREN, don't do that!" said the teacher.

"It won't come out," said Nellie. "It's *stuck*."

The teacher tried to get Nellie's finger out, but he couldn't.

Neither could the principal.
"It's stuck," they said, and sent Nellie home.

"It's stuck," said Nellie.
"I can get it out," said Henry.
"Mom!" shouted Nellie.

But Mom couldn't get Nellie's finger out.
"I can," said Henry.

So Mom called the doctor.
"I can't get it out," he said.
"I can," said Henry.

So the doctor called the police.
"We can't get it out," they said.
"I can," said Henry.

So the police called the magician.
"I can't get it out," he said.
"I can," said Henry.

So the magician called the farmer.
"I can't get it out," said the farmer.
"I can," said Henry.

So the farmer called the firemen.
"We can't get it out," they said.
"I can," said Henry.

Nobody could get Nellie's finger out.
Her nose was longer, and it hurt.
There was only one thing left to do.

"I can get it out," said Henry.

So everybody called the scientist.
"Of course I can get it out," he said . . .

. . . "Science can do anything."
And he measured Nellie's nose.
"I can get it out," said Henry.

So the scientist built a rocket, and tied it to Nellie's arm.

Then he tied Nellie's leg to the park bench.

Then he set off the rocket,

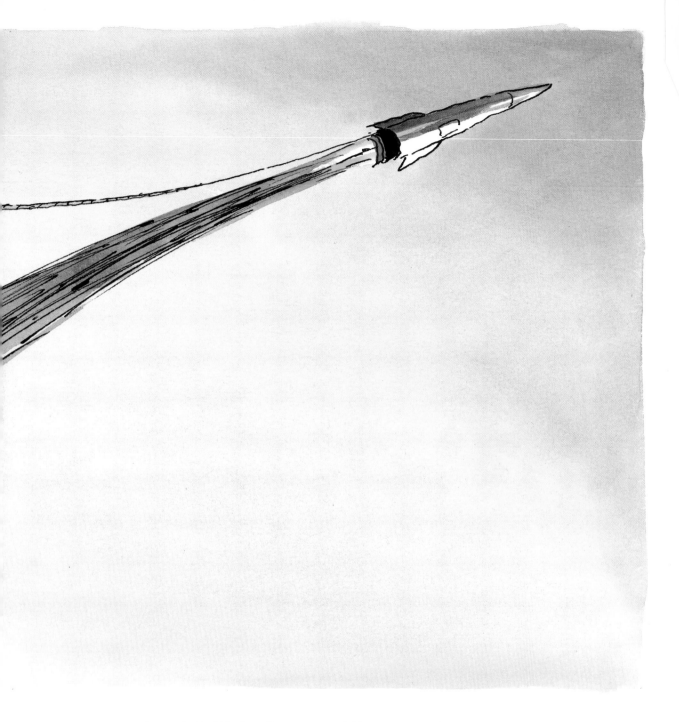

. . . but Nellie's finger *still* wouldn't come out.

"I can get it out," said Henry.

"Go on then!" said the teacher, the principal, Mom, the doctor, the police, the magician, the farmer, the firemen and the scientist.

So Henry tickled Nellie...
...and it worked!

The
end →